Make friends with

The little pony with the big heart

Sheltie is the lovable little Shetland pony with a big personality. His best friend and owner is Emma, and together they have lots of exciting adventures.

Share Sheltie and Emma's adventures in

SHELTIE THE SHETLAND PONY
SHELTIE AND THE RUNAWAY
SHELTIE IN DANGER
SHELTIE LEADS THE WAY
SHELTIE AND THE STRAY
SHELTIE AND THE SNOW PONY
SHELTIE FOR EVER
SHELTIE GOES TO SCHOOL
SHELTIE IN DOUBLE TROUBLE
SHELTIE AND THE FOAL
SHELTIE RACES ON

Peter Clover was born and went to school in London. He was a storyboard artist and illustrator before he began to put words to his pictures. He enjoys painting, travelling, cooking and keeping fit, and lives on the coast in Somerset.

Sheltie and Emma have lots of fans. Here are some of their comments:

'I love reading Sheltie books so much because I like the ponies and their exciting adventures.'

'You can't put the Sheltie books down until you have finished them because they are so good.'

'Sheltie always gets up to mischief and it makes me feel excited and scared!'

'I think people learn a lot more about ponies when they read Sheltie books because they tell you a bit about how to look after them and also how much fun they can be.'

Sheltie Rides
to Win

Peter Clover

PUFFIN BOOKS

PUFFIN BOOKS

Published by the Penguin Group
Penguin Books Ltd, 80 Strand, London WC2R 0RL, England
Penguin Putnam Inc., 375 Hudson Street, New York, New York 10014, USA
Penguin Books Australia Ltd, 250 Camberwell Road, Camberwell, Victoria 3124, Australia
Penguin Books Canada Ltd, 10 Alcorn Avenue, Toronto, Ontario, Canada M4V 3B2
Penguin Books India (P) Ltd, 11 Community Centre, Panchsheel Park, New Delhi – 110 017, India
Penguin Books (NZ) Ltd, Cnr Rosedale and Airborne Roads, Albany, Auckland, New Zealand
Penguin Books (South Africa) (Pty) Ltd, 24 Sturdee Avenue, Rosebank 2196, South Africa

Penguin Books Ltd, Registered Offices: 80 Strand, London WC2R 0RL, England

www.penguin.com

Sheltie Rides to Win first published in Puffin Books 1998
Sheltie and the Saddle Mystery first published in Puffin Books 1998
This edition published 2002
2

Copyright © Working Partners Ltd, 1998
All rights reserved

Created by Working Partners Ltd, London W6 0HE

The moral right of the author/illustrator has been asserted

Filmset in 14/22 Palatino

Made and printed in England by Clays Ltd, St Ives plc

British Library Cataloguing in Publication Data
A CIP catalogue record for this book is available from the British Library

ISBN 0–141–31390–0

Contents

Sheltie Rides to Win

To John Thorne

Chapter One

Emma quickly finished her breakfast. She spread far too much marmalade on her toast and crammed it into her mouth.

'For goodness' sake, Emma!' said Mum. 'Slow down or you'll choke.'

'Sorry, but I'm in a hurry,' said Emma. 'I'm meeting Sally at half-past nine and I'm already late.'

'Well, I'm sure Sally will wait five minutes. Now slow down!'

Mum raised one eyebrow as she spoke. That meant there was to be no argument. Emma gave a big sigh and settled down. She couldn't help feeling so excited. She had felt that way ever since she first saw the poster two days earlier.

One of Emma's favourite things to do with Sheltie, her little Shetland pony, was to sit in the saddle holding the reins loosely in her hands and let Sheltie lead the way. She liked to see which way Sheltie wanted to go and enjoyed being taken for a ride.

Two days ago, Sheltie had chosen to cross the stream. First he clip-clopped over the little stone bridge. Then he walked on and stopped further along at the village green, right next to a big colourful poster pinned to the village noticeboard.

There was a picture of a pony on the poster, and Emma read the words:

LITTLE
APPLEWOOD'S

FIRST
PONY
SHOW

Emma had never felt so excited in her life. And that was why she was rushing her breakfast.

Emma was meeting Sally and together they were going to ride into the village and put their names down on the entry register for the show. They wanted their names to be the first two on the list. Emma shivered with excitement just thinking about it.

After breakfast, Emma went bounding down the garden path. Sheltie blew loudly through his nostrils and dashed around the paddock in a wide circle. His eyes shone brightly as Emma palmed him a peppermint treat.

'Now, no messing about, Sheltie,' warned Emma. 'I want to get you tacked up and off. Do you hear?'

Sheltie nodded his head, then playfully decided to pull at Emma's T-shirt.

Ten minutes later, Emma and Sheltie were trotting down the lane on their way to meet Sally and Minnow.

Sheltie whinnied and flicked his tail

from side to side when he saw Minnow up
ahead.

Minnow was a larger pony than Sheltie.
He was black and white, with a long white
mane. Sheltie and Minnow were the best
of friends.

Minnow gave a loud whinny in reply, as
if to say, 'Hello, Sheltie. We're here.'

Sally greeted Emma with a big grin. 'I'm
so excited,' she said. 'I hardly slept a wink
last night.'

'Neither did I,' said Emma. 'Nothing
like this has ever happened in Little
Applewood before. It's our big chance to
show everyone what Sheltie and Minnow
can do.'

Chapter Two

Emma and Sally were a little disappointed when they arrived at the village green. Alice Parker and her two snooty cousins, Melody and Simon, were the first in the queue.

These days Emma was quite friendly with Alice Parker at school. Alice hadn't always been very nice. She used to make fun of Sheltie and call him names. That was before Sheltie had rescued Alice from a cliff-top in Summerland Bay and things had changed. Now Alice and Emma smiled and spoke to each other.

But her two cousins, Simon and Melody, were far worse than Alice had ever been. They looked at everyone down their noses all the time and were always cheating and playing nasty tricks on people.

Sally glanced at Emma and pulled a face. She knew Alice's cousins too. Sally remembered her first day at school, when Melody had pulled her hair and then stood there with Simon, laughing. Sally didn't like them one bit either.

Sheltie looked around. He hadn't met the other three ponies before and sniffed and nuzzled in a friendly way.

Alice Parker's pony was called Blue. He was happy to be friends with little Sheltie.

9

But the cousins' ponies! Well, they were as stuck up and as snooty as their owners.

Mrs Linney sat behind a trestle-table on the village green. The registration book was spread out in front of her. Raising funds for the Redwings Horse Sanctuary was Mrs Linney's idea. She had organized the entire pony show.

Mrs Linney looked up and smiled when she saw Emma and Sheltie. She was very fond of both of them. In fact, Mrs Linney used to look after Sheltie before Emma moved to Little Applewood.

Alice Parker and her two cousins registered their names and entered all six events in the show.

'I bet Melody and Simon think one of them will win the special trophy for the rider with the most rosettes,' said Emma.

'They've got to beat us first though!'
said Sally.

As the cousins rode off, Alice smiled at
Emma. But Melody and Simon didn't even
look her way.

'Walk on,' said Melody. And Simon
followed, leading their ponies away as
quickly as possible.

Now it was Emma and Sheltie's turn.
Sheltie lunged forward and knocked the
registration book off the table. Then he
pushed his nose close to Mrs Linney's face
and tried to lick her cheek.

'Oh, Sheltie!' laughed Mrs Linney. 'You
never change, do you?'

Sheltie blew a fat, noisy raspberry, and
Emma giggled.

'Have you chosen which events you
want to enter?' asked Mrs Linney.

Emma looked at Sally and grinned.

'Yes. We want to enter everything too! But we don't want to compete against each other because we're friends. We'd like to divide the events and enter as a team. We're going to call ourselves the "Saddlebacks".'

Mrs Linney smiled. She was only too

happy to enter both girls as a team. After all, it was to be a fun day and not a proper gymkhana. Mrs Linney thought there would be a few others who would want to do the same.

'The Saddlebacks it is then,' she said. 'I've put you down for all six events: the egg-and-spoon race, the potato race, the flag race, the bending course, the obstacle race and best show-pony contest.'

Mrs Linney told Emma that the special trophy for the winner with the most rosettes was to be a silver statue of a pony.

Emma and Sally made up their minds there and then that the Saddlebacks would try their hardest to win that trophy.

Mrs Linney wished them both luck and handed them two sponsorship forms. The next job in hand was to find willing sponsors to donate money towards the Redwings Horse Sanctuary.

It wasn't fair for both Emma and Sally to ask the same people for donations, so the two girls decided to split up.

Emma's first stop was Mr Crock, who was in his vegetable garden. As they trotted down the lane, Sheltie peered over all the stone walls. He liked sticking his neck into people's gardens.

However, when they got to Mr Crock's cottage, there was a surprise waiting for them. Alice Parker's cousin Melody was standing in the garden talking to Mr Crock.

Simon was holding Sapphire's and Midnight's reins and waiting out in the lane. When Sheltie saw them he let out a terrific snort. Simon wasn't holding the reins tightly enough and the two ponies were so startled that they pulled free and began to trot away. Without Melody and Simon in their saddles to stop them, the two ponies disappeared down the lane.

Chapter Three

The cousins were furious.

'Look what your stupid pony has done!' yelled Simon.

Then Melody said something rude to Emma and called Sheltie a big hairy ape.

Sheltie shook his mane and watched the snooty pair chase off down the lane after their ponies.

'Funny pair, those two,' said Mr Crock.

'Cheeky with it too. Wanted five pounds each for taking part in some charity races.'

Emma explained all about the Little Applewood pony show that Mrs Linney was putting on.

She told Mr Crock how friends and family were sponsoring riders in various events. And how all the money collected was going to the horse sanctuary.

'There's even a special trophy for the rider who wins the most rosettes,' said Emma.

'Well,' said Mr Crock, 'that explains it much better. I didn't trust those other two. But you and Sheltie, well, that's a different matter. Sheltie is worth five pounds of my money any day,' he said. 'But you make sure he wins those rosettes!' Then he signed Emma's form and gave Sheltie a carrot.

Emma's next stop was Marjorie Wallace and her brother, Todd. It had been some time since Emma and Sheltie had been visiting. Both Marjorie and Todd were very fond of animals and only too pleased to see Emma and sponsor her in Little Applewood's first pony show.

Mudlark the donkey came up to the fence and gave a loud bray when he saw Sheltie.

'Oh, look,' said Marjorie. 'Mudlark has come to wish you both luck.'

Sheltie gave one of Mudlark's long ears a lick and the little donkey nuzzled him, happy to see his friend again.

The rest of the morning proved very successful. By lunchtime, Emma had

fifteen names on her sponsorship form.

Emma was feeling very pleased with
herself. And Sheltie seemed to be more
excited than ever at the thought of being
in a pony show.

*

Later that afternoon, when Emma met up with Sally, they discussed their training plans.

'We've only got one week to get Sheltie and Minnow up to scratch,' said Emma.

Minnow would probably have been ready to enter the show the following day. But Sheltie! Well, Emma thought he needed quite a bit of work.

It wasn't as though Sheltie wasn't as clever as Minnow. Sheltie was very clever. Sometimes he was too clever.

Sheltie did everything that Emma asked him to do. The difficulty wasn't in getting Sheltie to *do* certain things. It was getting him *not* to do certain things. Or worse still, getting him to *stop* doing them, particularly when he was in one of his naughty moods.

But Emma hoped that with a little practice, Sheltie would be ready to prove to everyone that he was the best pony in the show.

Chapter Four

The next day was bright and sunny. It was Sunday, and Emma could hear the church bells in the distance as she skipped down the garden path and fastened the strap of her riding hat under her chin.

Sheltie was waiting patiently by the paddock fence.

'Oh no!' said Emma when she saw him. 'Just look at you!'

Emma could see that Sheltie had been

rolling in the paddock. His coat was covered in dry, dead grass. Several twigs were still hanging from his mane.

'Oh, Sheltie. What am I going to do with you?'

Sheltie took a nibble at the padlock and chain. Already he was frisky and ready for some fun.

'Mrs Linney is coming this morning, Sheltie. And now it looks as though I've got to tidy you up first!'

Emma climbed over the gate and began pulling the twigs and grassy briers from Sheltie's coat. Sheltie thought this was great fun and tried to pick the flowers on Emma's jumper with his teeth!

But Emma was having none of it. She was determined to clean Sheltie up before Mrs Linney arrived.

Emma ran to fetch a dandy brush and a hoof pick, along with Sheltie's saddle and bridle, and worked hurriedly to have him tacked up and looking presentable.

Sally arrived on Minnow minutes before Mrs Linney pulled up in her battered old car. As usual, Minnow was perfectly groomed, with every hair in place.

Mrs Linney clambered out of her car and gave Emma a wave.

Emma unlocked the gate and held on to Sheltie's reins while Mrs Linney carried a bundle of bamboo canes from the boot of her car into the paddock.

Sheltie was eager to greet both Minnow and Mrs Linney. He blew a series of loud snorts then nudged at the bamboo bundle in Mrs Linney's arms as Emma closed the gate. Mrs Linney almost dropped the lot.

Mum and Dad came down from the cottage with little Joshua and watched as Emma and Sally helped Mrs Linney to mark out a course with the bamboo canes. She poked them into the ground three paces apart in a long straight line.

'Right!' said Mrs Linney. 'First the bending course. What you have to do is to walk Sheltie through the line of canes, weaving in and out of each one without touching any. Take your time and make Sheltie work for you, Emma. You too, Sally. Make Minnow walk slowly in and out of the canes.'

Sheltie went first. He was very good at this even though he had never tried it before.

Sheltie didn't touch one cane until he came to the end. Then he deliberately

pushed his nose forward, grabbed the last
marker and pulled it clean out of the
ground.

'Never mind, Emma. Trust Sheltie!' said
Mrs Linney. 'But that was a brilliant first
attempt.'

Minnow was also good at this event. He
was a larger pony, so he wasn't as quick as

Sheltie. But he did finish the course without knocking any markers down. Or pulling any out!

Sheltie's second attempt didn't go very well at all. He could weave through the markers quite easily. But now he thought the best part was pulling out the canes. This time he removed three.

Mum turned to Dad and smiled. 'Sheltie is funny, isn't he?' she said. 'He knows perfectly well what he's supposed to do. He just likes messing about. Poor Emma. She's going to have her hands full.'

Emma whispered a few words in Sheltie's ear. And after several more attempts he finally grew tired of pulling out the canes and concentrated on weaving in and out beautifully.

The first time he made a perfect run

Emma gave Sheltie a peppermint. This seemed to make a lot of difference. Suddenly, Sheltie could fly through the markers without touching a single cane.

But Emma agreed with Sally. Minnow might be more reliable on the bending course. Sheltie couldn't really be trusted not to play.

Chapter Five

Next, Emma and Sally had some fun with the egg-and-spoon race. Mrs Linney had brought along two hard-boiled eggs to practise with.

'On the day of the show,' said Mrs Linney, 'the eggs won't be boiled, so they'll have delicate, fragile shells.'

It wasn't as easy as it looked either. Riding along with an egg balanced on a spoon was pretty tricky, especially at a fast pace. And each time Emma's egg fell to the ground, Sheltie tried to roll it around and play with it.

But Sheltie did have a really fast walk, and Emma's hand was very steady too, so Sally agreed that Sheltie would do better than Minnow in this event.

After egg and spoon, they practised the flag race. This involved taking flags which were stuck into the ground, then dashing with them one at a time at a mad gallop to an empty bucket about fifty metres away.

Sally and Minnow were really fast and very good at this race. Sally was happy to have this as one of her events.

The potato race was similar. The difference was that in this race you needed to dismount to pick a potato out of the bucket. And your aim had to be really good otherwise the potatoes came bouncing out of the bucket at the other end.

Sheltie didn't like eating potatoes, so he left them alone. But he did manage to kick a bucket over twice. However, being a little Shetland pony he was nearer to the ground than Minnow. And this gave Emma a better aim. Emma could also mount and dismount quicker.

Sally agreed that the potato race should be one of Emma's events.

'I've never seen anyone get on and off a pony so fast!' said Sally. 'I'm tired out just watching you.'

All this practice was thirsty work. Dad made some tea and poured three drinks for Emma, Sally and Joshua.

Sheltie and Minnow were nibbling at

the grass beneath the shade of a tree when
suddenly Sheltie looked up. He stared
right across the paddock out into the lane.

Sheltie was interested in something.
Emma glanced over to where he was
looking and saw Melody and Simon. They
were spying through a gap in the hedge.

When they saw Emma looking over
they kicked their ponies on and trotted
away up the lane.

Emma turned to Sally and said, 'Did you see those two?'

'Who's that?' asked Dad.

'Alice Parker's cousins. They were spying on us.'

'Don't be silly, Emma,' said Mum. 'They were probably just out for a ride and were interested in what you were up to.'

'Spying,' mumbled Emma under her breath. She didn't trust those two and neither did Sally.

When they had finished their drinks, Mrs Linney explained the obstacle race and the best-show-pony contest.

'The obstacle race is exactly that,' said Mrs Linney. 'A series of obstacles, bending canes and small jumps, with some tricky hazards along the way. Like walking through a line of flapping washing, treading over a sheet of black plastic, or passing a brightly painted dustbin.'

It sounded very easy to Emma, but some ponies didn't like surprises or things which flapped and rustled in the wind.

Emma knew that Sheltie would be brilliant at this. Nothing scared Sheltie. He was the bravest pony in the world.

Minnow was more timid than Sheltie but would be ideal for the best-show-pony contest. After all, Minnow was a proper show-pony and Sally was an excellent rider.

By the time Mrs Linney left, the two girls had worked out the races and events that would suit Sheltie and Minnow best.

Sheltie and Emma would compete in the egg and spoon race, the potato race and the tricky obstacle race.

Sally and Minnow would take the bending course, the flag race and enter the best-show-pony contest. Everything was settled nicely.

All that remained was a week of practice.

Chapter Six

After school on Monday, Sally rode over on Minnow to practise with Emma and Sheltie. They set up the bending canes which Mrs Linney had left for them to use and practised for an hour before teatime.

Although the bending course wasn't one of Sheltie's events, Mrs Linney said there would be some bending canes set out as part of the obstacle race.

Mr Crock had given Emma a sack of

potatoes to practise with for the potato race.

'Those potatoes won't even be good enough for chips after you've finished with them, Emma,' laughed Mum.

'They'll make good mashed potatoes though,' said Emma. Her aim was improving, and she found that if she tossed the potatoes into the bucket gently, without throwing them too hard, then they didn't bounce out again.

Sally and Minnow were getting really fast in the flag race too. Minnow's quick turns were perfect for this event.

Emma was still practising with a hard-boiled egg for the egg-and-spoon race. She knew it was going to be more difficult on the day with a fresh egg, but Mum had said, 'I'm sorry, Emma. I can't spare a dozen eggs each night just for practice.'

But she did help Emma to set up some small jumps and obstacles. She laid out plastic sheets and things for Sheltie to step over in preparation for the obstacle race. But Mum wasn't too pleased when Emma opened the paddock gate and started practising in the garden, with her clean washing hanging on the line.

Sheltie liked the way the shirts and tea towels flapped around his head as he dashed through them. But then he got tangled up in the washing with a shirt sleeve wrapped around his head.

'Emma! Tell Sheltie to stop doing that!' Mum yelled from the kitchen window as Sheltie pulled a T-shirt right off the line.

'Tomorrow I'll hang out a line of old

towels for you to practise with,' said
Mum. 'But until then, leave my washing
line alone!'

Melody and Simon had ridden over
once again. This time they'd brought their
ponies right up to Emma's garden wall.

Melody sneered and looked down her
nose as she said, 'You don't think you
stand a chance of winning anything on
that little scruffbag, do you?'

39

Emma was upset.

'Don't take any notice,' said Sally. 'They can't see past their own stuck-up noses. Sheltie's beautiful and everyone else who knows him thinks so too!'

Emma brightened a little. Yes, she thought. Sheltie is cute and clever, and on Saturday they would show Melody and Simon just how good he really was.

Emma took a deep breath. 'If you're so confident then why do you keep spying on us?'

It was Simon's turn to sneer now. 'Just thought we'd check out the competition,' he said. 'But we can see now that we don't have any!'

Then he dug in his heels, turned his pony and they both trotted away.

Chapter Seven

The next evening, after school, Sally came over again as planned. This time they practised together for the best-show-pony contest. Even though this was to be Sally's and Minnow's event, Emma and Sheltie joined in.

First, they walked the paddock. Then they trotted round in a perfect circle, keeping close to the fence. They practised walking forwards for six steps, then stopping before walking backwards.

'Walking backwards is tricky, isn't it?' said Emma.

At first Sheltie kept going backwards too fast and Emma found it difficult to make him stop after six steps. Minnow on the other hand did exactly what Sally asked of him.

'You'll soon get the hang of it, Emma.' Sally leaned forward and rubbed Minnow's neck.

They practised turning tight circles. Then they practised standing absolutely still without moving. Sheltie was brilliant. Normally, he couldn't stand still for long without fidgeting and jangling his reins. But he had been training really hard and stood perfectly still for fifteen seconds. Even when a bumble-bee buzzed around

his head, Sheltie didn't move. He just
watched it until it flew away.

'Well done, Sheltie!' said Emma. She felt
so proud of him and leaned forward to
give him a kiss.

Emma couldn't wait to show Melody
and Simon just how wrong they were
about Sheltie.

*

The rest of the week passed really quickly, with one hour's training every night after school.

On Friday evening, the night before the pony show, Emma didn't feel like eating anything at all. Butterflies danced in her tummy and she felt sick.

'It's probably nerves,' said Mum. 'You're just worrying too much about tomorrow.' She tucked Emma up in bed nice and early to get a good night's sleep before her big day.

Emma lay awake for ages. Every time she closed her eyes she kept seeing Melody's and Simon's snooty faces.

What upset Emma most though was that they thought Sheltie couldn't do anything because he was small. And that they laughed at Sheltie because his coat wasn't smooth and shiny like their ponies'.

Emma didn't care about that. She liked Sheltie's rough, shaggy coat and his long tail and mane. Still, she decided to get up extra early in the morning and give Sheltie a really good tidy up.

Emma finally went to sleep thinking of Sheltie and dreamed of him galloping free with his mane blowing in the wind.

Chapter Eight

In the morning, Emma leaped out of bed, crossed to the window and drew back the curtains. It was a beautiful, bright sunny day. A perfect day for a pony show.

Sheltie was standing in his usual spot by the paddock gate. Emma could see from the window that Sheltie had been rolling in his straw. A big clump of it was stuck to his forelock, right between his

ears. Sheltie looked funny, as though he was wearing a straw sunhat.

Emma laughed and felt all tingly inside. She hugged herself to keep the excitement from bursting out. Then she got dressed quickly in jeans and a T-shirt before making her bed and rushing downstairs.

As soon as Emma opened the kitchen door and looked out, Sheltie became frisky. He did a little stomping dance then shook his head, tossing his mane so hard that the straw flew off in a shower of golden strands.

Emma had at least one hour before breakfast time to get Sheltie ready. First his coat and then his tail and mane.

Sheltie seemed to know that it was a special day and was on his best behaviour. For once, he stood absolutely still and seemed to enjoy the grooming as much as Emma did. He even let her put on his hoof oil without a protest.

By the time she had finished, Sheltie looked neat and tidy, with a handsome, floppy forelock and bright, shiny hoofs.

Emma fed Sheltie his breakfast then

raced back to the cottage for her own. But before she did she gave Sheltie a stern warning: 'NO MORE ROLLING!'

Everyone seemed to arrive at the village green together. A covered canopy had been set up and a huge banner was strung between two trees. 'Little Applewood's First Pony Show' was painted across the banner in bold red letters.

Beneath the canopy was a long trestle-table which held the winners' rosettes and the impressive silver trophy. Mrs Linney sat at the table with a long list of competitors' names in front of her.

Mrs Fairbright, the vicar's wife, was also there alongside Mr Price, who was Emma's headmaster at school. They were both wearing big badges that said 'Judge' on their lapels.

Emma leaned forward and gave Sheltie's thick neck a good hard pat. Sheltie was interested in everything going on around him and wanted to make friends with everyone.

Emma felt very smart in her navy-blue riding jacket and white jodhpurs. Mum had bought the jacket specially for Emma to wear at the show. It was second hand and the sleeves were a little too long. Emma had to roll them up a bit, but she didn't care. She felt like a proper horsewoman.

Sally had on a blue riding jacket too, so they looked like a real team. Emma felt certain that the Saddlebacks would do really well.

As Emma and Sheltie waited in line to sign in with Mrs Linney, Emma looked around at the other riders and people at the show.

She saw Mr Crock, and Marjorie and Todd Wallace. She saw Alice Parker on her pony, Blue, and gave her a wave. Alice mouthed 'Good luck' and Emma gave her a nod and grinned. She also spotted Melody and Simon and quickly looked away.

Mum and Dad were there. Joshua was sitting high on Dad's shoulders and waved both hands like a windmill as soon as he caught sight of Emma and Sheltie. Emma beamed him a big smile, then blew him a kiss.

Suddenly Emma and Sally were next in line at the front of the queue.

It took some time for all the riders to sign in. But soon everyone was ready and Little Applewood's first pony show was about to begin.

Chapter Nine

'Will all riders in the egg-and-spoon race take up their positions, please.' Mrs Linney's voice boomed through a megaphone and called the competitors to the waiting area at one end of the green.

Everyone whose name was called walked their pony up to the starting line. There turned out to be too many to run in one race, so the contestants were divided into two groups.

Melody and Simon were together in the first group. Emma and Sheltie were in the second group with Alice Parker and Blue. The first five ponies to finish in the first group would race against the first five from the second group.

Each of the riders was given a spoon and a nice fresh egg. The first group of contestants stood in a neat line with their eggs balanced on their spoons waiting for the starting signal.

Mrs Linney swished a flag and they were off!

Ten ponies raced down the length of the village green at a fast walk. The crowd yelled and cheered as eggs got dropped and smashed. Riders screamed with excitement as they urged their ponies forward towards the finishing line.

Melody and Simon were in the lead.
Melody's pony, Sapphire, was really fast.
She was almost into a trot, yet the egg
stuck to Melody's spoon as though it were
glued.

Emma was amazed. It was going to be
very difficult to beat Melody and Simon.
Then, just before the finishing line,
Simon's egg popped out of his spoon and
smashed on the grass.

He was out of the race and Melody took
first place on Sapphire.

Ten more ponies lined up at the start.
They were given eggs on spoons and
waited for Mrs Linney's flag.

Emma was feeling pretty nervous and
had to concentrate really hard to keep her
spoon steady.

Mrs Linney swished her flag and the

race was on. Alice Parker and Blue were
the first away.

Sheltie only had short little legs but he
could move them really quickly. Sheltie's
fast walk was almost the same speed as
his trot.

There were three other ponies ahead of him and Sheltie started to walk faster and faster.

Then Blue went over a bump and Alice's egg leaped out of her spoon. Emma held her spoon steady as Sheltie put on a final spurt and crossed the finishing line in third place.

That meant that Emma and Sheltie would be racing again against Melody's Sapphire and eight other ponies.

'You were fantastic,' said Sally. 'Sheltie was going like a rocket!'

Emma smiled, but inside her tummy the butterflies were dancing again. The truth was she felt more nervous than ever when she lined up again for the final race. She patted Sheltie's rump and concentrated on holding her spoon steady.

Emma and Sheltie were standing next to
Melody and Sapphire. Melody sat with
her spoon at arm's length and looked
down at Emma with a smug expression.

'You might as well give up now, with
shorty,' she said, looking at Sheltie with a
horrible sneer. Emma took no notice, but
Sheltie did. Without any warning he
tossed his head sideways and knocked the
spoon out of Melody's hand.

The strange thing was that, as it fell, the
egg stayed in the bowl of the spoon. And
the egg didn't break when it hit the
ground either. It stayed in the spoon as it
lay on the grass.

Mrs Linney took two steps over and
bent down to pick up the spoon. She'd
seen what had happened. Melody's egg
was hard boiled and there was a little blob

58

of chewing gum sticking it to the bowl of her spoon.

Mrs Linney put both the egg and spoon into her pocket and handed Melody another spoon and a fresh egg. She raised her eyebrows as she looked straight at Melody and said sarcastically, 'Try again with these, dear.'

Melody's face turned bright red.

Emma smiled to herself and whispered, 'Well done, Sheltie,' under her breath.

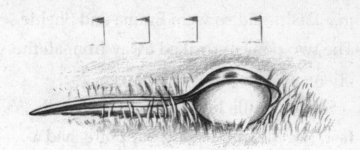

Chapter Ten

Emma and Sheltie stood at the starting line.

The flag swished and all the ponies shot forward. Melody and Sapphire were away in a flash. And so were Emma and Sheltie. The two ponies streaked away from all the others and flew down the green.

Sheltie's little legs were moving really fast. But Melody's pony, Sapphire, had a much longer stride and soon Melody was in the lead.

'Go on, Sheltie!' yelled Sally. 'Go on, Emma!'

Sheltie was now neck and neck with the larger pony. The finishing line approached. Sheltie stormed past in first place, with Emma still balancing the egg on her spoon. Sheltie had won!

In a temper, Melody threw down her spoon. Her egg smashed on the grass as Mrs Linney announced through the megaphone: 'The winner is Emma Matthews on Sheltie, riding for the Saddlebacks.'

Emma felt so proud. She leaned forward and gave Sheltie a big hug.

'You think you're really clever, don't you?' Melody snapped at Emma. 'You and shorty were just lucky, that's all.'

'We won fair and square,' said Emma. It

was her turn to be smug now, and Emma
enjoyed every minute of it.

Mr Price looked very pleased when he
pinned a red winner's rosette to Sheltie's
bridle.

'Well done, Emma,' he said. 'And well
done, Sheltie.'

Sheltie looked across at Melody and blew a loud raspberry. Melody pulled a face and stuck out her tongue.

The next event was the bending course. This event was set against the clock, with points lost if any of the markers were touched.

Sally and Minnow did really well, but took second place to Simon on Midnight.

'Never mind,' said Emma. 'You did your best. And you were both brilliant.'

Sally smiled. She felt really pleased even though she hadn't won.

Next was the potato race and, by this time, Sheltie was eager to have another go at something.

As before, there were two rounds and once again Emma and Sheltie found themselves in the final round-up against Alice Parker and her two cousins.

Alice seemed to be enjoying the show. But Melody and her brother Simon kept whispering together and staring over at Sheltie. They gave Emma the creeps. She didn't like either of them one bit. And neither did Sheltie.

The winner of the potato race would be the first rider who tossed five potatoes into their empty bucket.

Everyone had a bucket full of potatoes at the starting line. Empty buckets sat twenty metres away ready for the potatoes to be dropped into them. This was Emma's favourite event.

At a swish of Mrs Linney's flag the race began.

Sheltie was in great form. He seemed to

be going at a hundred miles an hour. All Emma's potatoes went straight into her bucket. Other riders were not so lucky. Potatoes were bouncing everywhere. And with everyone dashing about it was difficult to know who was winning.

Emma had four potatoes in her bucket already and was just about to drop in a fifth when she heard Melody shout 'I've won!'

Mrs Fairbright blew a whistle and everybody stopped.

Emma couldn't believe it. None of her own potatoes had missed, yet she was certain that she had seen at least two of Melody's go bouncing out of her bucket. Emma thought that she had been well ahead of Melody.

Sheltie seemed to think so too. He was

staring at Melody and making loud
snorting sounds.

Melody was laughing and looking at
Emma with her arms raised up in the air.
Emma looked down into Melody's
bucket. There were five potatoes there all
right.

But Sheltie couldn't stop staring at the
sleeves of Melody's riding jacket. One of
them looked particularly lumpy.

When Melody finally lowered her arms
to receive the winner's rosette, Sheltie
decided to take a better look. He grabbed
hold of Melody's sleeve and gave it a tug.
And out popped two potatoes for
everyone to see. They bounced on to the
grass at Mrs Fairbright's feet. Melody had
been cheating again!

Emma was the only rider with four

potatoes in her bucket. So the winner's
rosette was given to Emma instead.

Mrs Linney had a quiet word with Mr
Price and Mrs Fairbright. Then they called
Melody over on Sapphire.

'If you can't play fair, Melody, I'm afraid
you will be disqualified from the show,'
said Mr Price.

Mrs Linney stepped in. She looked very stern and said, 'We've decided to give you one last chance, Melody. So just behave.'

Melody pulled a face, then kicked her heels and stormed off on her pony.

As she passed Emma, Melody hissed. 'It's your fault, Emma Matthews,' she said. 'I'll get you for this!'

Chapter Eleven

The pony show continued.

The next event was the flag race. Straight away, Melody was up to her tricks again. She kept deliberately crossing in front of Minnow and confused Sally by dropping her flags into Sally's bucket instead of her own.

Then Melody started yelling, 'You're a cheat, Sally Jones!'

Everyone heard and this put Sally off.

Although she tried really hard and made a terrific effort, Sally only managed to finish in second place. Simon won the race on Midnight. That meant he had won two races and was now equal with the Saddlebacks.

'I can't believe that Melody,' said Emma. 'She cheats at everything.'

'I know,' agreed Sally. 'But she's really sneaky, isn't she? She made that one look as though it was my fault.'

'We'll have to keep an eye on her, won't we, Sheltie?' said Emma. Sheltie nodded his head then shook out his mane with a snort.

Nearly all the riders were having a go at the obstacle race.

The most difficult part was getting the ponies to walk through the flapping washing line and across the rustling plastic. Most of the ponies shied and took fright. One pony absolutely refused to go anywhere near either obstacle.

Emma spoke gently in Sheltie's ear. She knew that Sheltie could do it. She told him so. Sheltie was fearless.

Now it was Emma's turn. So far the best time for completing the entire course was two minutes and twenty-eight seconds.

Mrs Linney swished her flag and Sheltie went into action. First, he stepped nimbly over six striped trotting poles which lay on the grass. Then he cleared three small jumps and turned at a marked tree.

Next they had a quick canter to the bending course. In out, in out, in out, in – Sheltie stopped for a second and looked at the last cane.

'Don't you dare,' said Emma as she
squeezed with her legs. Sheltie hurried on
and left the cane alone. 'Phew!' breathed
Emma, relieved.

They raced on to the dreaded black
plastic sheet, but it was no problem for
Sheltie.

Emma was a little worried about the

washing line. She thought Sheltie would
be tempted to tug at one of the tea towels.
'Please, Sheltie,' Emma whispered. 'No
larking around.'

But Sheltie was having so much fun that
he didn't need to mess about, and passed
through without even a glance at the
flapping washing.

Sheltie took another jump over a small
bale of hay, then trotted past a fearsome
looking dustbin tied with balloons, and
dashed straight past the finishing line.

Brilliant! Sheltie and Emma had clocked
up the fastest time yet.

'One minute, thirty seconds,' screamed
Sally.

Emma felt so pleased. Sheltie blew
through his lips and snorted, tossing his
mane and holding his head high in the air.

'Your time is going to take some beating,' smiled Sally.

In fact, no one else came even near until it was Simon's turn.

Simon and Midnight were riding last. It seemed almost impossible, but they clocked up exactly the same time as Emma and Sheltie.

The judges decided to award both Sheltie and Midnight a winner's rosette. That meant that both Emma and Simon had three rosettes each in the competition for the special pony-show trophy.

There was only one event left to go. Sally and Minnow were up against Simon and Midnight for the best-show-pony contest. It was up to Sally and Minnow to win the final rosette to secure the special trophy for the Saddlebacks.

Poor Sally was feeling so nervous.

'Just do your best,' said Emma. 'It won't be the end of the world if we don't win the trophy, Sally. But it would be nice to beat Simon.'

'I know Minnow can win, Emma,' said Sally. 'I just wish I could stop shaking!'

'Just pretend that you're practising in the paddock,' suggested Emma. 'You were fantastic yesterday. Try to forget the crowd and concentrate really hard.'

Sally smiled and sat up straight in the saddle.

Then disaster struck. A terrible thing happened. As Sally walked Minnow over to the arena he stumbled and put his foot in a hole. When he pulled his foot out he had lost a shoe.

'Oh no!' said Sally.

Emma rushed over on Sheltie to see what had happened.

'I don't believe it,' said Emma. 'Minnow won't be able to compete now!'

Emma held Minnow's horseshoe in her hand and Sally looked tearful. She was so disappointed.

'I'm sorry, Emma,' said Sally, trying not to cry.

'It's not your fault,' said Emma. 'It can happen at any time. But what do we do now?'

There was only one answer: Emma and Sheltie would have to step in at the last moment and take their place.

'You and Sheltie can do it, Emma,' said Sally. 'I know you can.'

'It's the standing still part that I'm worried about,' said Emma. 'We've been training really hard, but Sheltie has never had to do it in front of all these people.'

But Sheltie was their only chance.

Simon looked over and gave a nasty sneer. Then he laughed when he saw Emma holding Minnow's shoe.

77

Melody was standing next to him. Simon whispered something to her and she disappeared into the crowd.

Chapter Twelve

Only eight ponies were entering for the best show-pony as it was such a difficult event. The ponies needed to be extremely well behaved and would be asked to perform various exercises.

Mrs Linney pulled the riders' names out of a hat to decide who would go first. Simon and Midnight were picked to perform seventh. Emma and Sheltie were drawn eighth – the last in the event.

Emma drew a deep breath. Eight was her favourite number.

Emma and Sheltie had to stand and watch all the other riders compete before them. She grew more and more tense.

Sally stood with Emma while the other riders went forward.

'Waiting around is the worst part, isn't it?' said Sally.

Emma nodded. 'It seems to be taking ages.'

Even Sheltie was getting restless. He jangled his reins and stamped his hoofs.

Then suddenly Sheltie became very interested in the overhead branches of a nearby tree.

'Oh, do keep still, Sheltie. Please!' Emma spoke softly and Sally palmed him a piece of carrot to keep him quiet.

Finally it was Simon's turn on Midnight. Mrs Linney started the clock and called out.

'First complete a neat, tidy trot in a wide circle around the arena.'

Midnight held his head high and looked like the perfect show-pony.

'Now take six steps backwards between the two bales of hay,' continued Mrs Linney. 'Then take six steps forward and turn a tight circle.' Midnight did both of these very well.

After that there was a figure of eight walking normally, ending with fifteen long seconds of standing still.

Finally, Midnight jumped over six cavaletti poles, cantered to a blue marker and stopped in front of the judges' table.

Simon and Midnight scored thirty-three

points. This was by far the best score in the competition.

Emma took a long gulp. 'That score is going to take some beating,' she said.

'I know. But if anyone can do it, you and Sheltie can,' said Sally.

Then it was Emma's and Sheltie's turn.

Mum came over and gave Emma a hug. 'Good luck, Emma. Just do your best!'

The crowd hushed to silence as Emma and Sheltie walked into the arena

Emma's heart was beating really fast as she took up her position and Mrs Linney set the clock.

Sheltie's circle in trot was perfect. He held his head proud and lifted his little legs high. The light breeze caught his long mane and it billowed out to the side.

Then Sheltie took six nervous steps backwards between the two bales of hay, followed by six confident steps forward and turned a perfect tight circle.

'Go on, Sheltie!' someone shouted. 'You show them!' It sounded like Mr Crock.

Emma grinned with pride.

Next was the figure of eight and

standing perfectly still for fifteen seconds.
This was the part Emma was dreading.

Emma counted the seconds away to
herself. She only got to four when
suddenly there was a loud bang. It
seemed to come from high in a nearby
tree.

Sheltie pricked up his ears.

Please don't move, thought Emma.
Then she heard the sound of a branch
snapping.

Before Emma could do anything to stop
him, Sheltie charged forward and rushed
over to the tree.

'Oh no!' cried Sally.

Sheltie stood beneath the tree and
looked up into the branches to where the
sound had come from.

Emma looked up too, and what she

saw made her gasp. Melody was high in the tree clinging to a broken branch. It looked very dangerous. Melody was about to fall at any moment.

Chapter Thirteen

Dad came rushing across the grass as Emma slipped out of the saddle.

'Quick, Dad,' said Emma. 'It's Melody.'

'Hold Sheltie still,' said Dad as he climbed up on to Sheltie's back. He stood on the saddle and reached up to help Melody.

'Somebody fetch a ladder!' he called.

Sheltie was brilliant. He kept absolutely still and didn't flinch or move a muscle.

One slip and both Dad and Melody would
come tumbling down. Dad was able to
support Melody's legs, but he didn't think
the branch would hold much longer.

Then, just in time, someone arrived with
a ladder. Melody screamed as the branch
finally broke away and crashed to the
ground.

Luckily, by then Melody was already on the ladder and Mr Price was helping her down.

The crowd cheered and Sheltie blew a ripple of noisy snorts.

'What were you doing in that tree, young lady?' asked Mr Price.

'Nothing,' said Melody, even though she had climbed up the tree and popped a crisp packet to scare Sheltie. But her plan had backfired and Sheltie had ended up saving her.

Melody was so embarrassed at being caught out that she burst into tears and ran away.

Because Sheltie's turn in the contest had been interrupted, he was allowed to start again.

This time Sheltie performed all the

exercises perfectly. Even the standing still part. All those hours of practice had really paid off.

There was a long silence as the points were totalled. Emma held her breath.

'Oh, Sheltie. Do you think we've done enough to win?' whispered Emma in Sheltie's ear.

At last Mrs Linney announced: 'Emma and Sheltie riding for the Saddlebacks have scored thirty-four points. The winner of the rosette is Emma Matthews on Sheltie.'

The noise was deafening. More whistles and cheers rang in Emma's ears. She had never felt so happy or so excited in her entire life.

Sheltie pawed the grass as Mr Price pinned a red rosette to his bridle.

'We're so proud of you both,' he said, beaming a big smile. 'Well done.'

Then a special announcement was made.

'The winners of the Little Applewood pony-show trophy are the Saddlebacks!'

Sally walked Minnow into the arena and joined Emma and Sheltie.

'Isn't it fantastic?' said Emma.

'We've won,' said Sally. 'We've really won!'

'And we beat snooty Simon and Melody fair and square. That was the best part,' smiled Emma.

The Saddlebacks received the special silver trophy. It was a pony galloping with its mane blowing in the wind.

'We can take turns looking after it,' said Emma.

Then they held the trophy between them and lifted it up in the air.

Alice Parker came over with Simon. She was pulling him by the arm. Simon just stood there. Then Alice gave him a nudge and he thanked Emma and Sheltie for rescuing his sister.

'Well done, Saddlebacks,' he added. The words seemed to stick in his throat.

Sally's father joined them in the arena. He was so thrilled about Sally and Emma's victory that he took out his chequebook and gave an extra donation to the horse sanctuary.

Now that the pony show was over, Sheltie was back to his cheeky self. He lunged forward and snatched the cheque from Mr Jones's hand.

'Don't you dare eat that!' said Emma.

Sheltie blew a noisy snort, which sounded like a laugh, and his eyes sparkled with mischief as only Sheltie's could.

Sheltie and the
Saddle Mystery

For Jenny, Peter and Daisy

Chapter One

Sheltie was all alone in his paddock. It was really quite early and Emma's Shetland pony had been awake for hours. It was too early for breakfast. And no matter how hard Sheltie stared at Emma's bedroom window from his favourite spot by the paddock gate, the bedroom curtains remained closed.

Every morning, Sheltie watched Emma's window and waited for her face to appear. But today she seemed to be taking ages. It had been raining almost non-stop for two days and Emma hadn't been able to take Sheltie out riding as often as usual.

The rain had stopped this morning, though, and the sun had broken through the ragged grey clouds. Everything smelt green and fresh. Sheltie felt frisky and alert. His nostrils twitched as he took in all the lovely country scents the rain had brought.

Sheltie had been cropping the grass for a good half-hour, but what he really wanted was his pony mix. The paddock was muddy, so Sheltie's feet and legs were covered with mud. He kept fidgeting and moving about, doing a funny little dance on the same spot. This only made matters worse and churned up the patch where he was standing even more.

Sheltie was getting bored. He tried a few loud whinnies and continued to watch Emma's window. But still nothing moved.

The little pony felt a sudden itch at his shoulder. He couldn't reach it with his teeth, so he decided to give himself a good scratch on one of the fence posts. There was a nice rough one, perfect for rubbing itches, at the far end of the paddock by the lane. Sheltie trotted over, squelching mud and grass beneath his little hoofs. He found the rough post and leaned against it with all his weight, rubbing and scratching.

Sheltie closed his eyes. That felt much

better. And as the little pony rubbed his itchy shoulder, the post moved. Only a fraction, but enough to make Sheltie's ears prick up. He rubbed a little harder. Then he pushed some more until the post really wobbled in the soft earth.

He knew that if he pushed just a bit harder the post would lean right over and there would be a little gap for him to squeeze through.

So Sheltie pushed. And there it was. A narrow space just wide enough for a little Shetland pony.

Once Sheltie was out in the lane he tossed his head and swished his long tail. It almost touched the ground, and swept through the muddy puddles as he splish-sploshed up the lane to find his own breakfast.

Sheltie knew exactly where to go. Mr
Crock lived at the top end of the lane and
was always up bright and early. Mr
Crock was a keen gardener and grew
heaps of vegetables in his walled garden.
There was always a carrot or two going
whenever Sheltie visited Mr Crock.

Halfway along the lane, Sheltie
stopped. A small, grubby green van

splattered with mud was rumbling towards him. Someone else was obviously awake and about their business. Sheltie didn't recognize the van. He had never seen it before. And when the van stopped and two people got out, Sheltie didn't recognize them either. One man was older than the other, but they were both rough-looking.

'Look at that!' said the younger man. He was no more than a teenager. 'A baby horse.'

'It's not a horse, stupid,' said the other. 'It's a pony. A little Shetland pony.'

'What's it doing out on its own so early, Dad?' said the younger man. (His name was Jim.) 'Let's catch it.'

But Sheltie had no intention of being caught. As the men approached, Sheltie pawed the ground and let out two loud snorts.

'He looks fierce,' said Jim.

'Fierce! You're not scared of a little Shetland pony, are you?' said Jim's father.

Then, as Jim made a grab for Sheltie, Sheltie lurched forward and charged past them, bowling Jim out of the way. Jim sat down with a bump, right in the middle of a muddy puddle. He was really cross and yelled, but his father laughed as Sheltie trotted away down the lane to Mr Crock's vegetable garden.

Sheltie was a very clever pony and an expert at slipping bolts. He unlocked Mr Crock's gate and nudged it open. Then he plodded into the garden and whinnied for Mr Crock, hoping for a nice juicy carrot.

Mr Crock heard Sheltie and came out of his potting shed.

'Good morning, Sheltie. You're up bright and early.' The old man looked around for signs of Emma. He guessed that Sheltie had escaped and was taking himself for a morning stroll.

'Have you been naughty again, Sheltie?'

Sheltie blew a raspberry. He could be so cheeky sometimes.

'Have you come for a carrot?'

Sheltie looked appealingly at Mr Crock and raised his hoof.

'Come on, let's find you one. Then let's get you back home. Emma will be worried out of her wits when she finds you missing.'

Chapter Two

Back at the cottage, Emma had just
woken up. It was the half-term holiday,
but she still got up nice and early.
Though not early enough today for
Sheltie. When Emma crossed to the
window and looked out into the paddock
she could see no sign of her little pony.

'Oh no!' said Emma.

She dressed really quickly and raced
down the stairs. Out in the garden Emma

called Sheltie's name. But Sheltie wasn't there to answer. She checked the fencing and soon found the gap where he had escaped.

Emma's heart missed a beat, but she knew where Sheltie would probably be. She began to hurry down the lane to Mr Crock's cottage. Halfway there she met Mr Crock walking Sheltie back the other way towards her.

'Sheltie!' called Emma. 'Where have you been?'

Sheltie blew a greeting and trotted towards her, his mane and tail bouncing. Mr Crock smiled. He didn't have to tell Emma what had happened. She knew exactly where Sheltie had been.

'I'm sorry if Sheltie has been a nuisance,' she said.

Mr Crock and Emma were friends. He
said he didn't mind early-morning visits,
but he was concerned that Sheltie had got
out of his paddock.

'Up to his old tricks, the rascal.' He

smiled and gave Sheltie a good pat, then said goodbye.

'Come on, Sheltie. Let's get you back home. You've given Dad some extra work to do now, haven't you?'

Emma's dad had taken a few days' holiday from work to do some odd jobs around the cottage. Now he had a paddock fence to mend as well.

Emma led Sheltie back to the cottage. She held on to Sheltie's mane and pretended she was a gypsy queen leading a wild pony in a fairy story.

She took Sheltie right up to the cottage. Joshua, Emma's little brother, came bouncing out all bright eyes and smiles.

'Hello, Sheltie,' he gurgled, and reached up to stroke the pony's soft velvety muzzle.

Sheltie stood very still and let Joshua stroke him. Mum looked out to see what was going on.

'Sheltie escaped,' said Emma. 'He pushed a fence post out and went to visit Mr Crock.'

'Oh dear,' said Mum. 'Looks like another job for Dad.'

She wasn't cross with Sheltie. He was such a lovable pony and it was part of his character to be naughty. Although sometimes it *was* a bother.

Emma fetched Sheltie's head collar and tethered him loosely to a ring in the stone wall of his field shelter. Then she gave him his pony mix to keep him occupied while she went inside for her own breakfast.

While Emma was busy shovelling

cornflakes into her mouth, Dad buttered some toast and relaxed with his newspaper.

After a few minutes he said, 'I don't believe it!' He looked up from his newspaper.

'What don't you believe?' asked Mum.

'This,' said Dad. 'Here in the paper. It says that there are rustlers in the area.'

'Rustlers! Here?' said Mum. 'Surely not. I thought rustlers only existed in the old Wild West.' She poured more tea.

'No. It appears that rustling still goes on, even in this part of the world. But in this case they seem to be stealing saddles rather than ponies. Especially new or expensive ones. According to the newspaper, three thefts have been reported in the last fortnight. One in Rilchester and two in Fenbury.'

'That's a bit too close to home,' said Mum.

'How awful,' said Emma. She felt really sorry for anyone who'd had their saddle stolen. 'Well, they'd better not try and steal Sheltie's, or I'll give them what for!'

'That's real fighting talk,' said Mum with a smile.

Emma spread a thick layer of strawberry jam on her toast. She was deep in thought.

'It would be so awful if someone stole Sheltie's saddle,' she said. 'I wouldn't be able to ride him properly. I'd have to go bareback.'

'There's no need to jump the gun, Emma,' said Dad, putting his newspaper down. 'I'm sure the thieves wouldn't be interested in Sheltie's old saddle anyway. Besides, it's so small. And there have been no reports of any thefts in Little Applewood.'

'But what about Sheltie's special

Sunday saddle? The one Marjorie Wallace gave him,' added Emma. 'That must be worth an awful lot of money.'

'Well, to be on the safe side, we'll just have to make sure the tack room is locked up every night, won't we? There, that's another job for you, Emma.'

Emma grinned and Dad went back to his newspaper.

He scanned the local adverts, then announced, 'This looks interesting.' There was an advertisement which read:

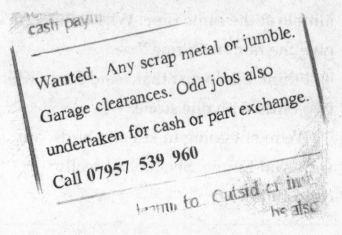

cash pay...

Wanted. Any scrap metal or jumble. Garage clearances. Odd jobs also undertaken for cash or part exchange.

Call 07957 539 960

...mu to. Outsid or in... he also

'I wonder,' said Dad. 'We've got a rusty old lawnmower that we don't use any more in the shed. And there's that old fridge and tin bath cluttering up the garage. The paddock fencing has quite a few posts that need mending. Perhaps we could clear out all our rubbish and get the repair work done in exchange.'

'There's my old sewing machine too,' added Mum. 'It would be a good exchange to have the paddock fencing fixed and get rid of all our clutter and jumble at the same time. Why don't you give the number a ring?'

'I think I'll do just that,' said Dad. 'Kill two birds with one stone.'

'We're not going to kill any birds, are we?' said Emma. She looked really concerned.

'Don't worry, Emma,' laughed Mum.
'Dad just means that we'll get two jobs
done at the same time. It's only a saying.'

Chapter Three

Dad telephoned the number in the advert straight after breakfast.

It was a mobile-phone number and a man answered it after four rings.

'Riley's Home Clearance and Repairs. How can I help you?'

Dad said that he had seen the ad, and explained the situation.

'The best thing to do is for me to come along and have a look. I'm sure we can sort out something, sir. Some kind of arrangement.'

Dad gave the address of the cottage and Mr Riley said he would be there within the hour.

Then Dad went out to the paddock with Emma to release Sheltie and to make a temporary repair to the fence. He took a length of rope from the shed and tied the fence post back into position.

Sheltie looked on sheepishly. Although he didn't understand that he had done anything wrong, he seemed to know that he was responsible for whatever it was that Dad was doing.

Emma looked at the state of Sheltie's coat and decided to hose down his legs. They were caked with mud from the paddock. Sheltie stood still and allowed

Emma to hose and sponge him down.
Then she gave him a brush, and a
peppermint treat for being so good.

An hour passed quickly and both Emma
and Sheltie looked up when they heard
an exhaust backfiring out in the lane. A
battered green van pulled up and

stopped outside the cottage. It was the same green van that Sheltie had seen earlier that morning.

Sheltie made a rumbling noise in his throat, then gave a loud snort.

'What is it, boy?' said Emma. Sheltie trotted over to the side of the fence where the van was parked. Mr Riley and his son climbed out.

Dad was inside the cottage with Mum, sorting out the cupboard under the stairs. The old lawnmower was already propped up outside the shed along with the tin bath.

'It must be the fence people,' said Emma. She raced inside to fetch her parents.

It took less than ten minutes for Mr Riley and his son Jim to view the collection of articles on offer: the lawnmower, the bath, the sewing machine, the fridge and an odd assortment of junk that Mum and Dad didn't want any more.

'Mmm . . .' said Mr Riley. 'It would be worth our while to come to some arrangement. Let's take a look at the work you need doing.'

Dad led the two men over to the paddock fence and pointed out the dodgy posts. There were four in all that needed fixing. One needed replacing altogether, with some repair work to the rails.

Sheltie followed Mr Riley and Jim as they walked around the paddock testing the various posts. He recognized them from earlier that morning when he had met them out in the lane. Sheltie remembered how they had tried to grab hold of him. He didn't like them one bit. His ears went back and he kept tossing his head.

The men ignored Sheltie, but Emma thought there was something wrong. And

when Sheltie began to paw at the ground with his hoof, Emma looked puzzled.

'What's wrong, boy?' she said. She stroked his furry face. 'It's only two workmen come to mend your paddock fence. Don't be nervous.'

But Sheltie wasn't nervous. He just didn't like these two men and nobody else seemed to notice.

Finally, Mr Riley said, 'I think we can certainly do a deal. If we take away all your rubbish, we'll do your repair work in exchange, plus an extra ten pounds.'

Mum raised her eyebrows. Dad smiled. Ten pounds seemed a very fair price to get rid of all that junk and to have Sheltie's fence repaired.

They shook hands and Mr Riley arranged to come back the following day with a bigger truck, to take everything away and start the work.

Everyone seemed happy except Sheltie.

The next day, Mr Riley and Jim returned with the truck. They loaded everything up, then set to work on the fence repairs. First they removed the old wobbly posts. Then they dug holes into which they were going to pour cement before refitting the posts. The paddock needed one brand-new post. The men were going to bring that along with the cement the next day.

They spent the rest of the afternoon hammering long nails into any loose rails around the paddock. By four o'clock they had finished that part of the work.

Meanwhile, Emma had to keep Sheltie

occupied and away from the gaps which the men had made in the fence when they'd dug the holes.

Part of the time, Sheltie had to be tethered in his field shelter. He didn't like that very much. But later on, when Emma's friend Sally and her pony, Minnow, came over, the two girls decided to take Sheltie and Minnow out for a long ride.

As they got ready to go, Mr Riley chatted to them while he packed up his tools. 'That looks like a very fine pony,' he said.

'I bet it costs a lot to keep a pony like that,' said Jim. 'What with feeding and the price of saddles and bridles and everything!'

Mr Riley smiled at Sally. 'I bet that

saddle cost your parents a fortune. It
looks like it's made of the finest leather.'

Sally felt pleased that they had noticed
Minnow's saddle. But Emma felt
uncomfortable. She suddenly
remembered the saddles that had been

reported stolen in the newspaper. She hurried Sally along.

When they were out and about riding through the countryside, Emma told Sally about the recent saddle thefts.

'That's awful,' said Sally. 'What a horrible thing to happen! Saddles are very special, aren't they, Emma? I've had mine ever since I've had Minnow. It was a special birthday present from my aunt. I'd hate to have it stolen. It's nicely worn in, and very comfortable for Minnow.'

'Well, let's hope the saddle thieves don't come round here,' said Emma. 'That's the last thing we need in Little Applewood!'

Chapter Four

The next morning, Mr Riley and Jim
arrived bright and early with the new
fence post and the cement.

Emma had arranged to ride over to Fox
Hall Manor to meet Sally and Minnow
and spend the day practising their
jumping. Sally had a nice little course of
jumps set up in her back meadow. Emma
loved riding there. She felt like an
Olympic rider taking Sheltie over proper

jumps. Back in Sheltie's paddock there were only old bricks and planks of wood to practise with.

When Emma arrived at the big wrought-iron gates of the manor, she saw Police Constable Green's Range Rover parked outside. The gates were open and Emma rode Sheltie through and round to the back of the house, where Minnow's stable was.

She dismounted and led Sheltie to the loose box. A soft whickering came from Minnow's stable. The pony stuck his head over the door and nuzzled Emma's hand as she reached out to stroke him. Then he greeted Sheltie with a little snort. Sheltie whinnied and tossed his head in reply.

'Where's Sally?' asked Emma.

Minnow didn't look very happy. Emma could tell that something was wrong.

Then Emma heard the sound of footsteps on the cobbles. Mr Jones, Sally's father, appeared from round the corner. PC Green and Sally were with him. Sally's eyes were red and her face was blotchy. She had obviously been crying.

'Hello, Emma,' said Mr Jones. 'I'm glad you're here. Perhaps you can cheer Sally up.'

Fresh tears welled up in Sally's eyes.

'I'm afraid someone broke into the tack room during the night and stole Minnow's saddle,' said Sally's father.

'Oh no!' gasped Emma. 'Poor Sally. You must feel awful.' She put her arms around her friend and gave her a hug.

Unfortunately this only made Sally start crying again.

PC Green said he would try his best to find the thieves and the saddle. 'But I can't say that I hold out much hope,' he added. 'There have been several reports of saddle thefts in the district lately, and we're pretty sure the villains move the saddles to other parts of the country to sell them.'

Mr Jones was very angry about the stolen saddle, but he knew that PC Green would do everything he could to find it.

'Thank you for coming over, constable,' he said. 'Let me know as soon as you hear anything.'

'Make sure your tack room is safely locked up each night, Emma,' said the policeman. 'We don't want to encourage this sort of thing in Little Applewood.'

Emma promised, then went back to trying to cheer up her friend. She decided that the best way to help was to be as cheerful as possible herself. Minnow came up to the stable door again and blew gently down Sally's neck.

'Don't worry, Sally,' said Emma. 'You'll get Minnow's saddle back.' But she didn't feel quite as sure as she sounded.

'I'd lend you Sheltie's Sunday saddle, but it would be too small.'

Sally forced a smile. 'There must be something we can do, Emma. That saddle was special. It was Minnow's and now it's gone!' Another tear trickled down her cheek.

Then Emma had an idea. 'I know what we can do to get your saddle back,' she whispered. The two girls exchanged glances. Sally knew that some of Emma's ideas were impossible, but she was willing to listen.

'Let's go into the meadow and ride bareback for a while. Then I'll tell you my plan.' Emma wanted to be out of Mr Jones's earshot. She didn't want anyone to find out what she was up to.

Sally slipped on Minnow's bridle and led him down across the lawn. Emma led Sheltie to the meadow and then took off his saddle. Then the two girls rode their ponies bareback.

Sally cheered up a bit and began to enjoy herself. She had never ridden bareback before. It took some getting used to, but felt really comfortable.

Then Emma told Sally her plan.

'We'll set a trap for the robbers and catch them red-handed,' she said excitedly. 'I bet they won't have got rid of Minnow's saddle yet. They probably have to steal several to make it worth their while. So let's encourage them to steal Sheltie's!'

Sally looked down at Sheltie's saddle lying on the grass.

'I don't mean to sound rude,' said Sally. 'But Sheltie's saddle is rather small and very old, isn't it? Minnow's saddle was as good as new.'

'Not *that* saddle, silly,' said Emma. 'Sheltie's special Sunday saddle. It's beautiful.'

'Oh no. You can't do that, Emma! What if it really *does* get stolen? You can't lose

Sheltie's Sunday saddle. It's *so* special.
It's got patterned work on it and must be
very valuable. Besides, it was a present
from Marjorie and Todd.' Sally sounded
very anxious about Emma's plan.

'But it might work,' said Emma. 'And
if it helps to get Minnow's saddle back
and catch the thieves, then it will be
worth it. Trust me, Sally. I have a feeling
this will work.'

When Emma was determined, nothing
could stop her.

'What we'll do is parade Sheltie's
saddle around the village so that
everyone can see it,' Emma explained.
'With any luck, the thieves will see it too
and they'll come snooping round to
Sheltie's tack room where we'll be
waiting for them.'

Sheltie gave a loud snort and nodded his head.

'Yes, but –' Sally began.

'No buts,' said Emma. 'It's what we've got to do.' She was already hot on the trail of the saddle thieves. Emma was now the great detective and eager to put the first part of her plan into action.

Chapter Five

'Supposing the thieves *do* see Sheltie's Sunday saddle and *do* come snooping round Sheltie's tack room. What then?' asked Sally. 'How will we catch them? They're probably big men and we're only little girls.'

'Easy-peasy,' said Emma. 'We'll ask if you can sleep over at my place. Then after dark we'll sneak out and keep watch on the tack room. If we leave the tack-room door unlocked, the thieves will go inside. Then we strike!'

'Strike?' said Sally. It was all beginning to sound dangerous. 'Are you going to hit them, Emma?'

'No, silly,' Emma said with a laugh. 'We'll just lock them in, then get Dad to telephone the police.'

It sounded too easy. Sally wasn't so sure about the plan, but she didn't want to disappoint Emma, especially if Emma was willing to risk Sheltie's special Sunday saddle.

'OK. That's settled then,' said Emma. 'Let's get started straight away. We'll go home and I'll saddle up Sheltie and show him off around the village.'

Emma and Sally walked Sheltie home. They didn't tell anyone what they were up to. Mr Jones was pleased to see that Sally had brightened up. And when she told him she was going over to Emma's cottage, he didn't mind one bit.

Emma's mum and dad were busy in the garden. Mr Riley and Jim were also busy setting the fence posts in concrete. But they did look up and stop working when they saw Sheltie with his special saddle.

'My, my, what a beautiful saddle,' said Jim. 'It's much nicer than his old one, isn't it?'

Sheltie blew a loud raspberry.

Emma grinned. 'It's Sheltie's special Sunday saddle,' she chirped. 'It's worth a fortune.'

'Well, you just make sure you take care of it then,' said Mr Riley.

'I will,' said Emma. Then she winked at Sally and led Sheltie off down the lane to the village, to tempt any would-be robbers.

The rest of the morning, Emma and Sally paraded Sheltie all over Little Applewood. Sheltie really enjoyed

himself, but they didn't meet anyone that they didn't know or trust. They saw Mr Crock, Fred Berry, Marjorie Wallace and Mrs Pinkerton from the corner shop. They saw Charlie from the garage and lots of other people too. But no suspicious saddle thieves.

Sally came back with Emma to the cottage. When Mum heard about Minnow's saddle she was upset for Sally and invited her to stay for lunch. Dad telephoned the Manor to let Sally's parents know where she was.

In the afternoon the two girls talked through the second part of the plan. Emma asked if Sally could sleep over. Mum said it would be all right as long as Mr and Mrs Jones agreed. Emma was certain the answer would be yes, especially as Sally was so upset about Minnow's saddle.

Dad drove Sally home to fetch an overnight bag.

Emma's next brilliant idea was to ask Mum if she could put her tent up in the bedroom.

'We can use the sleeping bags and camp out inside,' said Emma brightly.

Mum thought it sounded like a fun idea and said she would help her. It was a metal-framed tent like an igloo and didn't need any guy ropes or pegs. It fitted perfectly in the space between Emma's bed and her wardrobe.

When Dad and Sally came back with Sally's things, the workmen were just finishing off in Sheltie's paddock. The posts were set and the concrete would harden overnight. All that was left for them to do was hammer the rails to the new posts the next day and the job would be complete. The gaps in the fence had been covered with temporary boards to stop Sheltie from escaping during the night.

Sheltie was very interested in all the work that had been going on and kept

looking at the new posts and tossing his head. And every time he saw Mr Riley and Jim he would snort loudly and his ears would go back. Emma was puzzled by Sheltie's strange behaviour. She couldn't understand why he didn't seem to like either Mr Riley or Jim. They were such nice, friendly people. But Sheltie thought differently.

Chapter Six

That night, Emma and Sally camped out in the bedroom as planned. Joshua wanted to sit in the tent with Emma and Sally for a while before he went to bed. Emma read him a story by torchlight until he was sleepy and Mum carried him off to his own bedroom.

The two girls sat up late, chatting and discussing their plan. When Emma's mum and dad had gone to sleep, Emma and Sally were going to creep downstairs and out into the garden. Emma was going to unlock Sheltie's tack room and then they would hide and wait for the saddle thieves.

Emma felt really excited. Sally was more nervous than Emma, but thrilled at the idea of an adventure, even though it seemed dangerous.

Finally, Mum and Dad came upstairs to bed. Mum looked in on Emma and Sally. The two girls pretended to be asleep. But they lay quietly awake until they were certain that Emma's parents were sleeping themselves.

Then Emma and Sally got dressed and crept downstairs and out into the garden.

The moon shone brightly, so it didn't

seem very dark at all. Emma unlocked the tack-room door. Then they found a place to hide in the shadows behind the shrubbery, and watched.

Sheltie saw Emma and Sally from his paddock. He blew a snort and became frisky, stomping his feet and swishing his long tail.

'Shh, Sheltie!' whispered Emma. But Sheltie wouldn't quieten down until Emma went over and gave him a stroke and ruffled his mane.

Sheltie watched Emma as she went back into hiding and stood on guard, keeping a keen watchful eye on their hiding place.

Sheltie knew that something was going on.

'Let's hope that the robbers saw

Sheltie's saddle and fall into our trap,' said Emma.

'I just hope I can stay awake,' said Sally, yawning.

'I'll make sure you do!' said Emma. She was wide awake and bursting with excitement. She so much wanted to catch

the thieves and get Minnow's saddle back.

The night was silent except for the odd hoot from an owl in one of the trees. A hedgehog snuffled around in the bushes near by and for a moment Sally was frightened. But Emma laughed and then Sally felt silly. Her tiredness wore off and she too became wide awake and alert. But nothing seemed to happen.

Some grey ragged clouds passed across the moon and the garden became dark and filled with shadows. It was spooky at first, but Emma knew that Sheltie was not far away. If anyone came snooping around, then Sheltie would snort and give them a warning. Sheltie stood with his fuzzy chin resting on the top bar of the wooden gate. His ears twitched at every noise, no matter how small.

More time passed and still nothing happened. Emma shone her torch briefly on to her watch. It was half-past one. The night ahead seemed endless.

The two girls kept awake by whispering their plan over and over. If the thieves came and went into the tack room, they would charge out together and push the door closed. A sliding bolt was fixed to the outside of the door, ready to be slipped across. They knew that they had the advantage of surprise. The thieves wouldn't be expecting anyone to leap out of the bushes and lock them in.

'But what if it all goes horribly wrong and they *do* manage to get away with

Sheltie's saddle?' worried Sally. 'What do we do then?'

Emma grinned. 'I've got a secret,' she said. 'Sheltie's saddle isn't in the tack room at all. I've taken it out and hidden it in the cupboard under our stairs.' Then she produced a big brass whistle. It was the old-fashioned kind that makes a lot of noise. 'If anything goes wrong I'll blow this. Want to give it a blow?'

Sally didn't. 'You'll wake your mum and dad up if you do. And then we'll be in *real* trouble!' But Sally did feel more confident knowing that Emma had the whistle. She was also glad that Sheltie's saddle was safe.

At half-past three the two girls decided that nothing was going to happen.

'It will be getting light in an hour or two,' said Emma. 'Looks like our plan hasn't worked.' Then she had another idea.

'We can make some posters advertising Sheltie's saddle for sale,' she explained. 'If we put them up all over Little Applewood then the thieves are bound to see them. And then they'll know for sure that there's a saddle worth stealing. I bet they won't be able to resist that!'

Emma went and said goodnight to Sheltie. She planted a big kiss on his nose and ruffled his forelock. Then Emma and Sally locked the tack-room door and crept back indoors and up the stairs to bed. Within minutes they were both fast asleep in the tent, exhausted.

*

150

The following morning Emma and Sally were still asleep when Joshua came bouncing into the room. He dived into the tent and the girls woke up with a start.

Emma sat up. 'What time is it?'

Sally rubbed her eyes and looked at her watch. 'It's just gone eight.'

'Come on, sleepyhead. We've got work to do!'

After feeding Sheltie and sitting down to their own breakfast, Emma and Sally set to work with felt pens and paper. They hid themselves away in the tent pretending to be playing explorers. They didn't want Emma's mum or dad to see what they were doing.

Joshua sat with them scribbling on a pad. He couldn't read what his sister was

writing, so it didn't matter that he was
there.

Emma and Sally made twenty posters.
Each one said:

Brand new leather
Saddle for sale
Worth at least £200.
Bargain at £50.

Underneath they had written the address
of Emma's cottage.

Chapter Seven

'Right,' said Emma. 'All we've got to do now is to stick these posters up all over Little Applewood. We'll take Sheltie with us to show off his saddle again. If this doesn't work, then nothing will.'

Sheltie looked up suddenly when he heard his name. He knew something was going on and pawed at the ground with his hoof.

Mum and Dad thought the two girls

were up to something, but didn't say a word. Sally didn't seem so unhappy any more, and they didn't want to spoil things.

Even when Emma asked if Sally could sleep over a second night and pitch the tent out in the garden, they didn't seem to mind.

Suddenly, Sheltie snatched one of the posters out of Emma's hand and raced across the paddock with it.

'Oh no!' said Emma. 'Quick, Sally, before anyone sees it.'

The two girls chased Sheltie in circles until he finally dropped the poster in exchange for a peppermint.

'Oh, Sheltie. You are so naughty!' Emma said, smiling.

Everything was set. Sally's parents had

said it was all right for her to stay over.
And Emma's mum had agreed to let
them move the tent out into the garden. It
was almost summer. There was no sign of
rain and the ground had already dried
out nicely. They could put up the tent

behind the shrubbery, where it wasn't far from the cottage, but couldn't be seen from the road.

That afternoon, Emma and Sally took Sheltie out and pinned up their posters all over Little Applewood. It would be impossible for anyone to miss them. All that remained was to be patient and wait until nightfall.

Emma crossed her fingers and held them up for Sally to see. Sheltie leaned forward to sniff them. Then he whinnied softly.

'Let's hope that the crooks take the bait and fall into our trap,' Emma said.

Sally smiled. Emma sounded like a television detective, hot on a case. She crossed her fingers too.

'Let's hope we can stay awake,' said Sally. Her mouth stretched open into a big yawn. 'We didn't get much sleep last night, did we?'

Sheltie was playing copycat. He lifted his head and opened his mouth, just like Sally.

Emma nudged Sally and made her jump. Emma laughed. 'That woke you up, didn't it?'

Sheltie snorted loudly and shook his mane as Sally grinned. 'You'll probably have to do that every five minutes,' she said.

Emma looked as though she was going to nudge Sally again. 'But not until tonight,' Sally added quickly. She didn't want to end up black and blue if it wasn't really necessary.

They went over to Horseshoe Pond for the rest of the afternoon. They took Sheltie with them and let him crop the grass as they sat beneath the sycamore tree watching the ducks on the water.

Sally hadn't brought Minnow with her and she missed him, but it was fun just sitting there and talking. Sheltie seemed to miss Minnow too and kept looking around for him and whickering softly.

It was almost teatime when they finally came back to the cottage. Mr Riley and Jim had finished the fence, been paid their wages and gone. Mum and Dad were both sitting at the kitchen table. In front of them, spread out across the table were at least ten of Emma's and Sally's posters.

When Emma saw their faces, she knew
that she was in big trouble.

Mum didn't want to cause a fuss in
front of Sally, but she asked about the
posters all the same.

'What is the meaning of these, Emma?'
she asked. 'Why on earth have you put
Sheltie's saddle up for sale? We've had
three callers at the cottage in the last half-
hour. Surely you can't be thinking of
selling Sheltie's special Sunday saddle.'

Emma had to think quickly. She hadn't
expected Mum and Dad to find out about
the posters. She hadn't even thought
about the possibility of anyone actually
turning up to buy Sheltie's Sunday
saddle. The posters were meant to tempt
the thieves. The plan had backfired!

'I'm sorry,' said Emma. 'It's just that

Brand new leather
saddle for sale
Worth at least £200
Bargain at £50

Sally was so sad when Minnow's saddle
was stolen. I wanted to help and –'

'It's a nice thought, Emma,' Mum
interrupted. 'But selling Sheltie's saddle
to help Sally buy a new one isn't a good
idea. And I don't think that Sally or her
parents would really approve of it either.'

'After all, Emma, Sheltie's Sunday

saddle is very special and it *was* a present,' added Dad.

Sally turned bright red. She didn't know what to say, so she said, 'They're right, Emma. It's a very kind thought, but it's a silly idea offering Sheltie's saddle for sale. You can't do it.'

Emma gave Sally a look.

'I'm sorry,' Emma said. 'After tea I'll go out with Sheltie and take down the rest of the posters.' It was a lovely evening and Emma could cover the area easily within the hour. She looked at Sally again and raised her eyebrows.

'Phew! That was a close one, Sally,' whispered Emma as they went up to her room. 'Let's just hope the thieves have seen the posters too, before I take them down.'

'I felt awful,' said Sally.

'Me too,' agreed Emma.

After tea, Emma went off with Sheltie to gather up all the other posters just like she'd said she would. She was suddenly worried that Marjorie or Todd might have seen them too. What would they think? Emma hadn't thought of *that* possibility either.

Sally stayed at the cottage and played with Joshua until Emma returned. No more was said about the posters. Mum and Dad didn't want to embarrass Sally any further.

Chapter Eight

Later that evening, when the sun had disappeared behind the hills, Mum made up a flask of hot chocolate and a little parcel of crisps and biscuits for Emma and Sally to take out to the tent.

'You might get hungry or want a drink later,' said Mum. She sat in the tent with the two girls for a little while after she had put Joshua to bed. Later, Dad came out too. It was cramped but cosy inside the tent. Emma felt like an adventurous explorer and was looking forward to sleeping out under the stars.

It was a really warm evening and the sky was clear. Dad said he would leave the outside light on all night although it wasn't really that dark at all. The moon was full and bright. It shone in the dusky sky like a big silver ball. The grass looked silver too. The moonlight shone on Sheltie's mane, making him look like a ghost pony.

The little Shetland pony stood by the paddock gate watching the tent. His eyes were bright and alert. Sheltie could just make out a small corner of it poking out from behind the shrubbery next to the cottage. He knew that Emma was inside and wouldn't take his eyes off it.

All was quiet and peaceful in the
garden as Emma and Sally curled up in
their sleeping bags and waited. They each
had a torch and Emma had her big brass
whistle. Neither of the girls felt sleepy.
They were both wide awake and far too
excited.

'Isn't this fun?' said Sally. For a
moment she had forgotten why they were
really there. Then she suddenly
remembered and her tummy did a

somersault. 'I think I'll have one of those biscuits,' she said.

When they were certain that Mum and Dad were fast asleep, Emma and Sally crept out of the tent and unlocked the tack-room door. They left it slightly ajar. It was a perfect trap to catch a thief.

'Whatever happens, don't lose that whistle, Emma,' said Sally. She was beginning to feel rather nervous.

'I won't.' Emma had threaded a piece of string through it and hung it around her neck. She patted the whistle. 'They'll hear this at Scotland Yard!'

Sheltie had seen them out in the garden and blew several loud snorts. He was stamping his hoof by the gate and making quite a lot of noise.

'Shh!' whispered Emma. She put a

finger to her lips but she knew that Sheltie wouldn't quieten down until she went over to pet him.

It was lovely being out in the moonlight with Sheltie. Emma gave him a hug and he soon settled down and kept watch as Emma joined Sally back in the tent.

Sheltie knew something exciting was going on.

Emma and Sally decided to take turns looking out for the thief. If they peeped out of a flap at the tent's entrance, they could see the tack-room door quite clearly. But after a while Emma decided to watch from behind the large water-butt which was nearer. After all, if anyone did come, it would be a long way to run from the tent to the open door. And they might not be able to catch the thief in time. They could also see Sheltie quite clearly from there, and it was nice to know that he was watching too.

Sally took first watch. If anyone came she was to throw some gravel over the bushes on to the tent behind. But midnight passed and nothing happened. When it was Emma's turn, she crept out of the tent and over on tiptoe to the water-butt. She found Sally fast asleep.

'Sally!' snorted Emma. 'You're a fat lot of good!'

'Whaa?' said Sally sleepily. 'Oh! Sorry, Emma. I nodded off.'

Emma took up her position in hiding and Sally dragged herself off to the tent.

'And for goodness' sake, Sally. *Stay awake!*'

Sally grinned sheepishly.

Although it was the middle of the night, Emma could still see very well because the moon was shining so brightly. Every time Emma peeped over at Sheltie, he shook his long mane to let her know he could see her. As Emma crouched, waiting for the crooks to appear, her heart was thumping so loudly that she was worried someone would hear it.

Ten minutes later, Emma heard a noise.

Sheltie heard it too and raised his head suddenly.

A grubby green van drove up the lane and stopped at the garden gate. Behind the van was a small trailer. Emma gasped. It was the saddle thieves. Emma was sure of it. They had come. But why had they brought a trailer?

Suddenly, the answer dawned on Emma. It was only too clear. The trailer was just big enough for a small Shetland pony. They were going to steal Sheltie as well as the saddle!

Emma felt awful. If the thieves took Sheltie it would be all her fault.

Emma could hardly breathe. She threw

the handful of gravel over the bush on to the tent. But Sally was fast asleep inside and didn't stir.

Two figures got out of the van. Mr Riley and Jim! Emma could see them both as clear as day.

Emma's mouth dropped open. So *they* were the saddle thieves. She didn't want to believe it. They'd seemed such nice, friendly people.

Emma glanced around for a sign of Sally. But Sally didn't come.

'Sally!' hissed Emma. She didn't dare call any louder for fear of being heard. Should she blow her whistle and run indoors and fetch Dad? Emma didn't know what to do.

Suddenly her plan seemed very foolish indeed. She hadn't thought for one second that Sheltie might be in danger of being stolen.

At that moment, Jim took a pair of sturdy wire-cutters and a halter out of the van and went over to the paddock gate. He quickly snapped the padlock chain, pulled the safety pin and slipped the bolt across.

Sheltie pawed at the ground and snorted noisily as Jim pushed open the gate. Jim went into the paddock and Sheltie galloped away to the far side. But when Jim went after him, Sheltie ran at him and Jim had to jump out of the way. It wasn't going to be easy to catch Sheltie.

'Leave the pony for a moment, Jim,' said Mr Riley. 'Let's get the saddle first. Then we can both go after the Shetland.'

Emma breathed a sigh of relief. At least

Sheltie was safe for the moment. But for how long?

Jim came out of the paddock and closed the gate. Then he followed his father and tiptoed to the tack room. The door was ajar only metres from where Emma was hiding.

Mr Riley pulled the door open and

went inside. Jim followed. They didn't switch on the light and it was pitch dark inside. But Emma saw a torch flash and two shadows appeared framed in the doorway.

'You're sure there are pickings here, Dad?' Emma heard Jim say.

'That saddle must be here somewhere,' grunted Mr Riley. 'Look behind those sacks.'

It was now or never. With a tremendous surge of energy Emma flew out of her hiding place.

Sheltie saw Emma rush to the door and push it closed with all her strength. Then she shoved the bolt across.

'Here, what's going on?' shouted Jim, and thumped on the door.

Emma needed help – urgently. Quickly

Sheltie leaned over the gate and undid the catch with his mouth. Then he nudged the gate open and rushed up the garden to the tack room. Emma was so pleased to see him.

Inside the tack room Mr Riley and Jim banged on the door and threw themselves against it. They cursed and shouted, 'Let us out!'

The window was barred, but the door didn't look very strong. The bolt was going to give way at any moment. Sheltie saw what was happening and leaned all his weight against the door. No matter how hard Mr Riley and Jim pushed and shoved, they couldn't budge the little Shetland pony. Sheltie stood there, determined not to move an inch.

'Good boy, Sheltie,' Emma said,

smiling. Then she took the whistle and
gave it several long, noisy blasts.

'What's that?' Mr Riley's face appeared
at the window. 'It's that girl and her
flipping pony. They've got us locked in!'

'OK,' said Jim. His face appeared next
to Mr Riley's. 'You've had your fun,

Emma. It was a good game. Now let us out and we can go home.'

Sheltie blew a warning snort and Emma wouldn't let them out. Instead, she blew the whistle again, and this time Sally came racing out of the tent. At the same moment the upstairs window flew open and Dad peered out.

'Come quickly, Dad,' shouted Emma. 'We've trapped them! Sheltie and I have caught the saddle thieves!'

To Emma's relief, Dad was downstairs and outside in seconds, with Mum running along behind him. It was all very well playing detective, but Emma suddenly realized how frightening and dangerous it was. If it wasn't for Sheltie standing guard, Emma was certain that the two men would burst through the door at any minute. And then what? Emma quickly told Mum and Dad what had happened.

'Emma, go back into the cottage with Sally and Mum, now! And telephone the police.' Dad sounded really cross.

He waited with Sheltie for the police to arrive.

Emma and Sally watched with Mum through the kitchen window.

Outside, Mr Riley and Jim were still trying to escape, but Sheltie was a very strong little pony and wouldn't budge.

Two policemen arrived in a Range Rover. It was PC Green and PC McDonald. Seeing them, Sheltie moved away from the door.

Mr Riley and Jim had given up any hope of getting away now, but made up a story that they were looking for some tools they thought they had left behind.

'Well, let's just take a look then, shall we?' said PC Green as he snapped handcuffs on to the two villains.

He flicked on the light. Inside, the tack room was empty. There was no saddle and no tools either. Just Sheltie's bridle and grooming brushes, along with a store of pony mix in sacks.

When PC McDonald looked inside Mr Riley's van, he found Minnow's stolen saddle. Mr Riley couldn't explain *that* away. The pair of them had been caught red-handed.

'You seem to have caught two very nasty rats in your trap,' said PC Green. He smiled at Emma and Sally and told them how foolish they had been to try and catch the thieves on their own without telling anyone. 'You should leave this sort of thing to the police!'

Dad wasn't too happy to hear about Emma's plan either. He was quite angry. 'You should have told us what you were up to, Emma. These two could have been very dangerous and you might have been hurt.'

Still, there was no harm done, and

Mum and Dad were very glad to have Emma safe and sound.

'We couldn't just sit back and let them steal people's saddles,' said Emma. 'They had to be caught.'

Emma fancied the idea of joining the police force herself when she grew up. She explained this to PC Green. 'And don't you think Sheltie would make a smashing police pony?' she added. 'He may be small, but he's very brave and clever. He's got a nose for trouble.'

'I can believe that,' said PC Green, and Sheltie gave him a playful nudge as he led the two culprits away.

'I'm afraid we'll need Minnow's saddle for evidence,' said PC McDonald. 'But we can let you have it back in a day or two, Sally.'

Sally hoped she wasn't going to get into too much trouble when her parents found out.

The next morning, Sally's father came over to the cottage. He sat down with Emma, Sally and Emma's parents, and gave the two girls a real telling-off.

But nobody stayed cross with them for long. After all, they had been clever to catch the thieves and promised that they would never do anything like that again. As a punishment Emma and Sally were to go without television for a whole week.

Later that morning, after Mr Jones had taken Sally home, Emma wrote a letter to Sally's parents to say that she was sorry for getting Sally into trouble. She took it to the Manor herself.

*

Sally got Minnow's saddle back after a
few days, and the two girls went riding
over to Barrow Hill.

Sally felt very happy to be back in
Minnow's saddle. She couldn't really
explain to Emma how awful it was to
have had it stolen. But Emma
understood. She remembered how
terrible she'd felt when she'd thought
that Mr Riley and Jim were going to take
Sheltie. That would have broken Emma's
heart. She leaned forward on to Sheltie's
neck and gave him a hug and a kiss.

'And to think,' said Emma, 'that I
put Sheltie in danger. I'll never do that
again – ever!'

'You know,' she said, 'we can see for
miles up here. All over Little Applewood.

This is the perfect spot for ponies on patrol. I know we're not old enough to join the police force yet, but we could keep an eye open for any trouble, couldn't we?'

'*Emma!*' said Sally. 'We promised.'

'We won't *do* anything. We'll just keep our eyes open, that's all. I'll be the chief

detective and you can be my trusty assistant.' Emma's grin spread wide across her face.

'I'll be second in command or I won't do it at all,' said Sally playfully, with a yawn. Emma reached over and poked Sally in the ribs.

'Same thing, isn't it?' she laughed.

Sheltie joined in with a funny snort that sounded a little like a laugh.

'Come on, sleepyhead, I'll race you to the stream,' said Emma.

Then she squeezed Sheltie with her knees and galloped away down the slope.